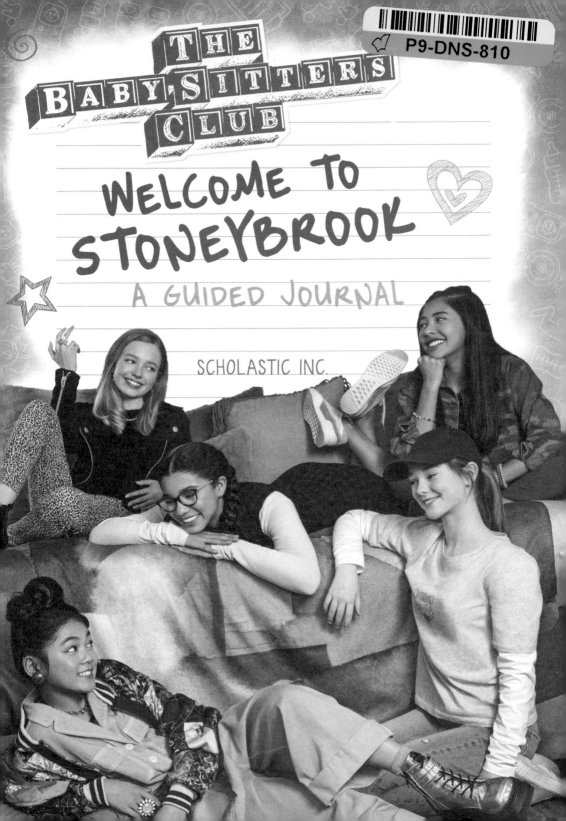

# THE BABY-SITTERS CLUB

# WELCOME TO STONEYBROOK

## A GUIDED JOURNAL

SCHOLASTIC INC.

All rights reserved. Published by Scholastic Inc., *Publishers since 1920*.
SCHOLASTIC and associated logos are trademarks and/or registered trademarks of Scholastic Inc.

The publisher does not have any control over and does not assume any responsibility for author or third-party websites or their content.

This book is a work of fiction. Names, characters, places, and incidents are either the product of the author's imagination or are used fictitiously, and any resemblance to actual persons, living or dead, business establishments, events, or locales is entirely coincidental.

ISBN 978-1-338-66512-3

10 9 8 7 6 5 4 3 2 1          21 22 23 24 25
Printed in the U.S.A.                     40

First printing 2021

Stock photos © Shutterstock.com

Written by Jenna Ballard
Book design by Jessica Meltzer and Marissa Asuncion

# Say Hello to Your Friends! ♡♡

The Baby-sitters Club is *the* go-to business for baby-sitting services in Stoneybrook, Connecticut. Whether it's a regular gig with the neighborhood kids or joining a family on their vacation to Sea City, Kristy, Mary Anne, Claudia, Stacey, and Dawn are ready for anything!

But that doesn't mean it's always smooth sailing. Forgetful parents, uncontrollable kids, a trip to the hospital, and a rival baby-sitting organization are just a few of the surprises these friends have faced along the way.

The surprises continue even when they aren't baby-sitting. Kristy's mom is getting married, Stacey has a serious secret, Claudia's passion for art just might bring her closer to her crush, and Mary Anne's dad and Dawn's mom are . . . flirting?! There's never a dull moment in Stoneybrook!

Learn more about your favorite BSC members, fill in the fun activities, and get creative by completing stories and writing prompts that put YOU in the world of the BSC!

If you were starting your own baby-sitters club with your best friends, who would be in charge? Who would keep the club organized? And, most important, who would provide snacks?

Check out the qualities of each officer position that follow, and then assign the roles according to which friend fits the description best. Don't forget to choose one for yourself!

## President

Some say bossy, some say natural-born leader. This friend has a take-charge attitude, runs the club meetings, and knows how to turn great ideas into action! She's a decision maker and the one everyone goes to in times of crisis.

My club's president is _____.

## Vice President

The VP is confident enough to cover for the president if she's not around but laid-back enough to let her take the lead the rest of the time. She provides important resources like a cool meeting space and keeps club morale high with delicious meeting snacks.

My club's vice president is _____.

## Secretary

This friend is the most organized person you know. The secretary is in charge of taking notes during meetings and managing the baby-sitting job calendar. She is reliable, pays attention to detail, and probably organizes her sock drawer by color and style.

My club's secretary is _____.

## Treasurer

Good with numbers is a must! This is the friend you turn to when you need help studying for that big math test. The treasurer handles club membership dues and any other money-related matters, so you know she's super responsible, too.

My club's treasurer is _____.

## Alternate Officer

This friend is totally adaptable and doesn't crack under pressure: the perfect choice to temporarily take on any of the other positions if a club officer misses a meeting. She's okay with jumping into new things without much warning or preparation—in fact, that's how she likes it!

My club's alternate officer is _____.

LOVE

# MEET THE BABY-SITTERS CLUB

## KRISTY

Position: President

Full Name: Kristin Amanda Thomas

Favorite Sport: Softball

Best Friend: Mary Anne Spier

The Baby-sitters Club was born from one of Kristy's most brilliant ideas (if she does say so herself). After watching her own mom struggle again and again to find a reliable sitter for Kristy's younger brother David Michael, Kristy thought: Why not make it easier for the parents of Stoneybrook? So Kristy turned her thought into a reality and founded the Baby-sitters Club.

Kristy has plenty of experience interacting with kids of all ages. (That's because she has two older brothers and three younger siblings, including her soon-to-be step-siblings Karen and Andrew.) With her active imagination, problem-solving skills, and practical experience, Kristy is a baby-sitter parents AND kids love!

"I'm bossy.
Get used to it."
—Kristy

As the president of the BSC, Kristy knows how to get things done! She has a vision for what she wants and then goes for it. But sometimes her no-nonsense attitude can rub people the wrong way.

Do you share any qualities with Kristy? Or do you know anyone who is just like her?

Pretty grate, I think. Good idea BTW.

**THE BABY-SITTERS CLUB®**

—Claudia

What is the name of your club? Use this space to try drawing some of your own logo ideas!

**My club's name is** _____.

# WOULD YOU RATHER?

## Baby-sitting Edition!

For each scenario, circle which one you would rather do if you HAD to choose!

### Would you Rather . . .

NO!

| | | |
|---|---|---|
| Baby-sit all eight Pike kids by yourself for one day | **or** | baby-sit the three rowdy Barrett siblings every day for a week? |
| Deal with a kid who cut off their own hair | **or** | one who scribbled crayon all over the hallway? |
| Take care of a baby who just won't stop crying | **or** | keep up with a hyper seven-year-old? |
| Watch twins you can't tell apart | **or** | a brother and sister who never stop fighting? |

OMG

123...

Play hide-and-seek for two hours straight

or

watch the same cartoon over and over?

Try to glue a parent's shattered vase back together

or

try to get a juice stain out of the carpet?

Change a smelly diaper

or

clean up after a kid gets sick?

The members of the BSC are best friends—but that doesn't mean they always get along. Kristy didn't trust Stacey when they first met, and Stacey thought Kristy was a bit, well, *intense*.

Even Kristy and Mary Anne, who have been next-door neighbors and BFFs since they were little, have had rough patches from time to time. The important thing is they always own up to making a mistake, and they show up for each other, no matter what.

**How do you deal with friendship troubles? How can you show a friend how much your friendship means to you the next time you fight?**

# Official Baby-sitters Club Meeting Minutes

By Mary Anne Spier, Secretary

Meeting #5

Wednesday

In attendance: Kristy Thomas (KT), Claudia Kishi (CK), Stacey McGill (SM), Mary Anne Spier (MAS)

## Jobs Booked:

* MAS for Karen and Andrew Brewer on Friday night. Job goes to MAS due to CK's and SM's Halloween plans (see below) and KT's general stubbornness re: Watson.

## Important Notice: Phantom Caller

* Home-invader story making the rounds on the local news (and unfortunately catching MAS's dad's attention, as if he doesn't already freak out enough).
* Caller makes anonymous phone calls, which are later discovered to be coming from inside the house. Creepy much??
* All baby-sitters be sure to check caller ID when out on jobs!

## Other Points of Discussion:

* Upcoming Halloween Hop
* CK and SM will be attending. KT states she would "rather have head lice."
* Trevor Sandbourne: Did he actually ask Claudia to go out with him or not? KT is skeptical of his intentions, but CK and SM aren't worried. Guys like Trevor Sandbourne don't just come right out and *ask* a girl to a dance. MAS wouldn't know, as interactions between her and a certain young male library volunteer have remained at a minimum.
* Possible costumes: Troll doll for CK—too baby-ish now that Trevor is her kind-of date? She will explore other options.

# BABY-SITTING BLUNDER

A great baby-sitter has to be ready for any situation that comes her way! The story is started for you below, but it can go anywhere from there. Use your imagination to finish the rest.

"Eight . . . nine . . . ten! Ready or not, here I come!" I shouted for the fifth time. Yes, five rounds of hide-and-seek with Buddy and Suzi Barrett and, somehow, I ended up being "It" Every. Single. Time.

I started with a few spots I could tell were empty to give them some extra time. After a few minutes I started looking for real, checking their favorite spots in the hall closet and under their mom's bed. No go.

*Well, after five rounds, it makes sense they're getting better at this*, I thought. But after ten more minutes of searching around the house, I was starting to get nervous. "Okay, you guys, you're too good for me!" I called out. "I give up! Show yourselves!" Nothing. I felt a weight in the pit of my stomach. Why weren't they answering?

123...

# MEET THE BABY-SITTERS CLUB

## CLAUDIA

**Position:** Vice President

**Full Name:** Claudia Lynn Kishi

**Favorite Books:** Nancy Drew mysteries

**Favorite Color:** Purple

Do you need a baby-sitter who loves to get creative? Someone who can color for hours, wow with origami sculptures, and isn't afraid of a little (or a lot) of glitter and glue? Look no further than Claudia Kishi, baby-sitter/artist-extraordinaire!

Art is a huge part of Claudia's life, from her fashion-forward style to her passion for painting. She loves to share her crafty hobbies with the kids she baby-sits, so she's guaranteed to bring tons of creativity to every adventure. And while Claudia is known to have quite the sweet tooth herself, she'll be sure to stick to every parent's preferred snack choices for their little ones.

"When I'm painting . . . all the little voices telling me what I should be doing and who I'm supposed to be go away. I feel calm. I feel like me."

—Claudia

_____
_____
_____
_____
_____
_____
_____
_____
_____
_____
_____
_____

Claudia is known for her totally unique sense of style. Choose an item from each row to build your own Claudia-worthy outfit!

Tops

Bottoms

Shoes

Accessories (Feel free to choose more than one!)

Now try your hand at fashion design by sketching your complete Claudia outfit here. Feel free to add a few personal touches—it's what Claudia would do!

# Stoneybrook Middle School
## Official Report Card

Student: Claudia Kishi          Grade: 7

*Whoops. Didn't think he noticed that.*

| Subject | Grade | Comments |
|---|---|---|
| English | B- | Teacher Comments: Claudia occasionally contributes insightful comments during class discussions, but she also spends a great deal of time doodling instead of reading. —Mr. Myers |
| Math | D | Teacher Comments: Claudia has potential, but she needs to apply herself more in class. —Mrs. Bradshaw |
| Science | C- | *Is anyone really suprised by this one?? Let's just except I will never be an acountent and move on.* |
| Social Studies | B- | |
| Gym | C | *Mrs. Donahue says my tie-die converse are to blame for how slow I run. Not the fact that, you know, I hate running.* |
| Art | A | Teacher Comments: Claudia is a pleasure to have in class! Her passion for creating and strong eye for design point to many more great things to come from this budding artist. —Mrs. Johanssen |

*If only all my teachers were as cool as this woman!*

# What would your teachers write on your report card?

For Claudia, art class is where she feels the most inspired to put in the work to make something amazing. But her parents wish she put that same dedication toward her math homework. Their priorities are different, and Claudia feels like she's always letting them down. Then Claudia discovers that her artsy crush, Trevor Sandbourne, feels the same way she does—even though his dad's an artist himself!

Write about a time when your dream or passion didn't line up with someone's expectations of you. Then write about a person who always supports you and encourages you to pursue what you love. Someone like Claudia's grandmother Mimi, who lets you know that you are enough—exactly as you are.

_____

_____

_____

_____

# "I'm proud of you because you are my Claudia."

—Mimi

What are some of your favorite inspirational quotes? Write them here and read them whenever you need a little boost.

# Quote #1

# Quote #2

# Quote #3

# TOP 10 HALLOWEEN COSTUME IDEAS

Complete the list with more killer costume ideas for the Stoneybrook Middle School Halloween Hop.

1. Tippi Hedren's character from *The Birds*

2. Marie Antoinette

3.

4.

5.

6.

7.

8.

9.

10.

What was your favorite Halloween costume you've ever had? What dream Halloween costume would you love to dress up in one day?

_____

_____

_____

_____

_____

_____

_____

_____

_____

_____

_____

_____

_____

# MYSTERY OF THE PHANTOM CALLER

**Finish the spooky story below!**

    I plopped down on the couch and let out a sigh. I had finally persuaded Jackie Rodowsky to go to bed after three stories, two trips to the bathroom, and two very thorough monster checks. I had about twenty minutes before Mrs. Rodowsky got home, so I turned on the TV. A local news anchor was reporting on a story about the Phantom Caller.

    "Two more Stoneybrook residents reported receiving anonymous, silent phone calls before valuable items inside their homes were stolen," the news anchor was saying.

    Then the phone rang. I froze. *Don't be silly,* I told myself. *It's probably Mrs. Rodowsky.* I went to the phone and picked it up. "Hello?"

    Silence. I gulped. "Hello? Who is it?"

    Still silence. Not even a dial tone. And then, suddenly, I heard it.

**CLAUDIA:**

Stace, u will never guess what Trevor Sandbourne just did

**STACEY:**

OMG what?

**CLAUDIA:**

He saw I was missing a paintbrush in art class and offered me 1 of his

**STACEY:**

Claudia!!!!!!!

**CLAUDIA:**

And when I said I would give it right back after class he said "don't worry about it, use it as long as u want"

**STACEY:**

You're basically dating now.

**CLAUDIA:**

Right?!?

Who's the first person you text when something exciting happens to you?

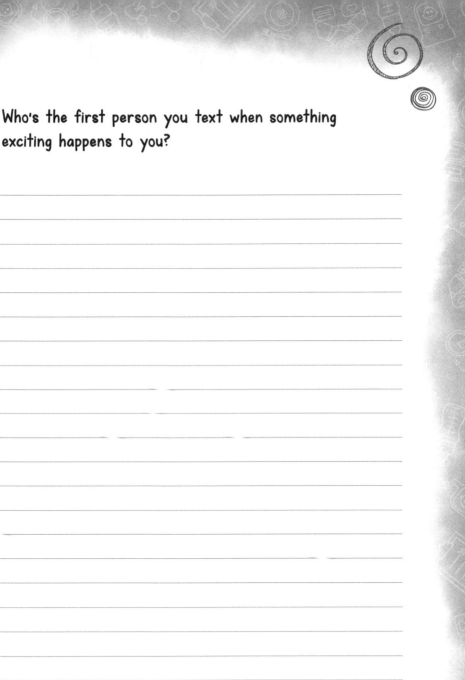

# BSC Weekly Job Schedule

| THURSDAY | FRIDAY | SATURDAY | SUNDAY | TBD |
|---|---|---|---|---|
| Stacey— Charlotte Johanssen | Kristy—Karen and Andrew Brewer (FINALLY) | Mary Anne— Eleanor and Nina Marshall | Mary Anne— Eleanor and Nina Marshall, take 2 | Newton baby?!?? Arriving any day now!!! |
| Claudia— Claire, Margo, and Nicky Pike | | | | |

Keep track of your own schedule for the week. Add your after-school activities, baby-sitting jobs, and family time. Don't forget your homework, too!

# Weekly Schedule

| MONDAY | TUESDAY | WEDNESDAY | THURSDAY |
|--------|---------|-----------|----------|
|        |         |           |          |
|        |         |           |          |
|        |         |           |          |

| FRIDAY | SATURDAY | SUNDAY | |
|--------|----------|--------|--|
|        |          |        |  |
|        |          |        |  |
|        |          |        |  |

# "What's a Kid-Kit? I'm so glad you asked."

—Kristy

When the baby-sitters need to stand out from their new competition, Kristy knows just the thing to set their club apart. The girls create Kid-Kits full of their favorite toys, games, books, and crafts to bring on every baby-sitting job. Doesn't every kid love the chance to play with someone else's stuff that's totally different from their own?

Kristy's Kid-Kit

Claudia's Kid-Kit

Mary Anne's Kid-Kit

Complete the list below with the things you would put inside your own Kid-Kit to become the most in-demand baby-sitter ever!

1. _____

2. _____

3. _____

4. _____

5. _____

6. _____

7. _____

8. _____

9. _____

10. _____

# MEET THE BABY-SITTERS CLUB

## STACEY

Position: Treasurer

Full Name: Anastasia Elizabeth McGill

Favorite Movie: *Mary Poppins*

Favorite Store: Barneys

Stacey McGill recently moved to Stoneybrook from New York City, so she can handle the hustle and bustle of a busy family household! Stacey is a girl of many baby-sitting talents. With her flair for fashion, she can pick an outfit for the fussiest of dressers in three minutes flat. And with her gift for numbers, she can help with math homework or make an educational game using just a few simple props.

Stacey also has diabetes. While it can be a difficult condition to manage, living with it has made Stacey very independent and responsible: two excellent baby-sitter qualities. She is always careful about keeping her sugar levels stable and monitoring how she feels. One thing is for sure: When Stacey is the sitter, it's healthy snacks only!

"That was when I realized I belonged. Not just to the club. Something bigger. A community. And they liked me just the way I was."

—Stacey

When Stacey first moved to Stoneybrook and joined the BSC, she kept her diabetes a secret from everyone—even Claudia. She remembered how she was treated by her so-called friends back in New York. She was afraid her new friends would treat her differently, too, once they found out. Luckily, Stacey couldn't have been more wrong. The BSC discovered the truth, but it only brought the girls closer together.

**What is one of your biggest secrets? Is there something about you that not even your best friends know? How do you think people would react if they found out?**

# STACEY'S TOP 10 SIGHTS YOU MUST SEE IN NEW YORK!

1. Barneys—department store or heaven???

2. Central Park

3. The Met

4. Levain Bakery (Just because I can't indulge in this sugary goodness anymore doesn't mean no one else should!)

5. SoHo (Did I mention I like shopping?)

6. Ballet at Lincoln Center

7. Bronx Zoo—the cutest giraffes!

8. Macy's Thanksgiving Day Parade

9. A Broadway musical

10. The Plaza Hotel (Who doesn't want to pretend to live in a hotel like Eloise?)

What are some of your favorite places in YOUR hometown?

_____

_____

_____

_____

_____

_____

_____

_____

_____

_____

_____

_____

_____

_____

_____

_____

_____

# Official Baby-sitters Club Meeting Minutes
By Mary Anne Spier, Secretary

## EMERGENCY MEETING. THIS IS NOT A DRILL.

In attendance: Kristy Thomas (KT), Claudia Kishi (CK), Stacey McGill (SM), Mary Anne Spier (MAS). Unplanned appearance by non-member Sam Thomas (ST).

## Important Notice: The Agency Is Moving in on BSC Turf!!!
* Lacy Lewis and other Stoneybrook High girls started their own club, the Baby-sitters Agency. (Sound familiar?)
* KT practically has steam coming out of her ears. She keeps ranting about some book called *The Art of War* and cutting off a snake's head . . .
* ST thinks the Agency sounds "pretty impressive." (MAS notes KT's expression and thinks ST should run for it if he knows what's good for him.)

## Strategizing:
* Agency advantages: fancy commercial, later curfews
* BSC advantages: We actually care about the kids we baby-sit. And it was our idea first!!
* Possible plans of attack:
    - BSC billboard in the middle of town (Need $$. Also: How does one buy a billboard?)
    - Convince all our parents to extend our curfews an hour (MAS already knows how that convo is going to go.)
    - ~~Create an attack ad against the Agency~~ (KT really needs to return that war book to the library.)

When the Baby-sitters Agency shows up and threatens to take over all the baby-sitting jobs in Stoneybrook, the BSC knows they have to do something to stay in the game. Brainstorm ideas in the list below to help the BSC stand out from their new competition!

# HOW TO SAVE THE BSC

1. _____

2. _____

3. _____

4. _____

5. _____

6. _____

7. _____

8. _____

9. _____

10. _____

Now pick your best idea from the list and design a flyer that will help the BSC win back their clients.

# MEET THE BABY-SITTERS CLUB

## MARY ANNE

Position: Secretary

Full Name: Mary Anne Spier

Hobby: Knitting

Favorite Animal: Kitten

Dependable. Responsible. Caring. Organized. These are the words everyone uses to describe Mary Anne. She's wise beyond her years and calm, cool, and collected in a crisis. A parent couldn't ask for a more reliable baby-sitter. Mary Anne may be quiet and sensitive, but she never hesitates to speak up and fight for what is right.

Mary Anne has a silly side, too! While the child's safety comes first, Mary Anne always makes sure they're still having a great time. Her specialty is reading great stories aloud before bedtime and perfecting the voices for each character.

"You can't always tell
from someone's outside
who they are on the inside.
But if you never ask them,
they never get a chance
to surprise you."

—Mary Anne

Of all the BSC members, Mary Anne is the quietest. Her oldest friends, like Kristy, expect her to be timid and shy all the time. But there's another side of her not everyone sees, like her quirky sense of humor. When Dawn moves to Stoneybrook, she befriends Mary Anne and helps unveil the parts of her hidden just below the surface.

Is there a side of you that most people don't see? What do you wish others knew or understood about you? It's never too late to reveal the real you.

# Sister,

You are cordially invited
to a New Moon Share-a-mony

### What you will discover:
Tarot readings, stargazing,
chanting, and an excellent cheese
spread (vegan options available)

Join your sisters to usher in the
New Moon, share your deepest thoughts,
and support one another during this time of
upheaval. Come with your favorite
crystals, ready to set an intention for
the coming month.

*Dawn wants me
to come to this with
her—do I dare?*

*Chanting???
I barely
sing in
the shower
because my
dad might
hear me.*

*Where would I even find a crystal?
Also: not so into this sharing idea.*

"So come forward. Share in this time of great transition! The universe is listening."

—Esmé Porter

_____
_____
_____
_____
_____
_____
_____
_____

Dawn and Mary Anne are up to a matchmaking scheme! Dawn's mom, Sharon, and Mary Anne's dad, Richard, dated in high school, and it's clear they still have eyes for each other. But it looks like they need a little help to push them in the right direction!

Help the girls finish writing a romantic letter from Mary Anne's dad to Dawn's mom. First, fill in the list without reading the letter. Then add the words from your list into the corresponding blanks in the letter on the next page and watch Richard's words come alive! (Whether Dawn's mom believes it's really from him is another story . . . )

Term of endearment _____

Verb ending in "ing" _____

Type of food _____

Adjective _____

Measure of time _____

Noun _____

My dearest _____,
(term of endearment)

Ever since you walked through my front door to join our

family Thanksgiving dinner, I haven't stopped

_____ about you. The moment our eyes met over
(verb ending in "ing")

the _____ I could feel that we still had
(type of food)

something special. I know it didn't work out between us all

those years ago because I was _____, but I
(adjective)

hope you're willing to give us another shot. I am counting

down the _____ until we can see each
(measure of time)

other again.


With _____,
(noun)
Richard

After Mary Anne heroically got Bailey Delvecchio to the hospital and made sure the nurses and doctors treated her right, people began to see that Mary Anne can be fierce and powerful. To celebrate Mary Anne coming to the rescue, Stacey made her a very special playlist.

## Mary Anne Is a Boss Created by: Stacey

**Track 1.** "Independent Women, Pt. 1" by Destiny's Child

**Track 2.** "Respect" by Aretha Franklin

**Track 3.** "The Greatest" by Sia

**Track 4.** "Defying Gravity" from *Wicked*

**Track 5.** "Brave" by Sara Bareilles

**Track 6.** "My Shot" from *Hamilton*

**Track 7.** "Shake It Off" by Taylor Swift

**Track 8.** "Run the World (Girls)" by Beyoncé

**Track 9.** "This Is Me" from *The Greatest Showman*

**Track 10.** "Mary Anne" by Boytoy

What are some songs that make YOU feel like a total boss? Create your own empowering playlist below to get you pumped up the next time you need a confidence boost!

# My Empowerment Playlist

Created by: _____

Track 1. _____

Track 2. _____

Track 3. _____

Track 4. _____

Track 5. _____

Track 6. _____

Track 7. _____

Track 8. _____

Track 9. _____

Track 10. _____

Mary Anne's total boss moment gives her the confidence to make some changes in her life, like trying a more grown-up style for her hair, clothes, and bedroom. But her changes aren't all on the outside. She also realizes that she needs to speak her mind and stand up for herself more often—even, sometimes, to her family and friends.

**What do you wish you were better at? How could you make some changes to help you work toward it, like Mary Anne does?**

# MEET THE BABY-SITTERS CLUB

## DAWN

**Position:** Alternate Officer

**Full Name:** Dawn Read Schafer

**Favorite Snack:** Homemade granola

**Hobby:** Speaking up and speaking out

All the way from the west coast, Dawn is the newest member of the BSC! But this California girl is no stranger to Stoneybrook. Her mother, Sharon, grew up here, and her great aunt is none other than the unforgettable Esmé Porter. Dawn grew up hearing her mother's childhood stories about Stoneybrook, and now she's looking forward to making some memories of her own.

Dawn is a big believer in accepting people for who they are and celebrating what makes everyone unique. What makes Dawn unique, you may ask? That would be her unconventional family, her passion for activism, and her trademark "California Casual" style. Dawn's positive attitude is an asset for any baby-sitting situation, and she can't wait to meet more of her new neighbors!

"Parents are just older weirdos, doing the best they can."

—Dawn

_____

_____

_____

_____

_____

_____

_____

_____

_____

_____

_____

_____

_____

_____

Dawn is super passionate about taking care of the environment. And from her vegetarian diet to her reusable straws, Dawn doesn't just talk the talk—she walks the walk and actually takes action to help!

What causes do you care about? Brainstorm some ways you could bring your passion to others and start taking action in your home, school, or community to make a difference.

## A cause that is important to me is

_____

_____

_____

## It is important to me because

_____

_____

_____

## Some people who might want to help with my cause are

_____

_____

_____

I can start making a difference in (circle one)

my home     my school     my community

by _____
_____
_____


I could share what I'm doing with
others by

_____
_____
_____

Much of Dawn's open-minded outlook on life came from her mom, Sharon. Ms. Porter is not your average parent. Although she can be a little, well, out-there, she taught Dawn everything she knows about being a strong woman and surrounding herself with a powerful circle of sisterhood.

Channel Dawn and her mom by writing a letter to a strong woman in your life—a friend, sister, mother, aunt, neighbor, teacher, anyone you want—and tell her why you think she's so amazing.

Dear _____,

_____

_____

_____

_____

_____

_____

_____

_____

_____

_____

_____

_____

_____

Places to Find in Stoneybrook

- Local farm share—ask Aunt Esmé
  which one she uses

- Ice cream—preferably with dairy-free options!

- Animal shelter—volunteer opportunity?

- Community yoga (maybe ask Kristy to join,
  too—she could use some breathing exercises)

- Nearest recycling center

- Fair trade coffee—for Mom

Moving can be hard. That's why it's important to find places that are familiar and will make you start to feel at home, just like Dawn does.

**What kinds of places would you turn to if you moved somewhere new?**

_____

_____

_____

_____

_____

_____

_____

_____

_____

_____

_____

_____

_____

# "We're both strong women with big personalities."

—Dawn to Kristy

Mary Anne and Kristy have been best friends forever. But when Mary Anne starts hanging out with Dawn, things get a little complicated. Dawn and Kristy never shy away from voicing their strong opinions— which means they sometimes clash with each other, leaving Mary Anne in the middle. Luckily, these girls learn that their fierce personalities make them more alike than different!

**Have you ever been stuck between two friends who disagree? How did you deal?**

Mary Anne and Logan clearly like each other. But sometimes their shyness takes over and they don't know what to say. Help Mary Anne express how she feels in this note to Logan. Complete each sentence by circling the word(s) you think sound best.

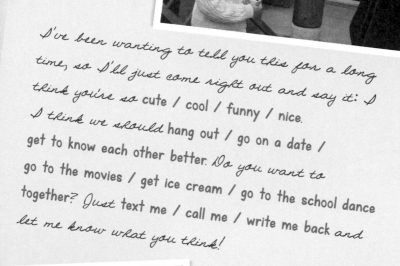

Logan,

I've been wanting to tell you this for a long time, so I'll just come right out and say it: I think you're so cute / cool / funny / nice. I think we should hang out / go on a date / get to know each other better. Do you want to go to the movies / get ice cream / go to the school dance together? Just text me / call me / write me back and let me know what you think!

Sincerely / From / XO,
Mary Anne

What are you too shy to say out loud to YOUR crush?
Try writing it in a note instead!

Claudia and her older sister, Janine, could not be more different. Claudia loves fashion and art while Janine loves coding and science. Claudia is all about feelings, and Janine is all about facts. Their rivalry only gets worse after Mimi's stroke. But as they watch Mimi's slow recovery together, they find a way to have a real connection—and maybe understand each other a little bit better in the future.

Do you have siblings or other family members you never see eye to eye with? Try to see things from the other person's perspective and think about ways you could learn to support each other.

"This is my sister, Janine. She hatched from a space pod my parents found in the compost bin and has struggled to adapt to the customs of Earth."

—Claudia

_____
_____
_____
_____
_____
_____
_____
_____
_____
_____
_____
_____

Sometimes what starts as teasing with siblings or close
friends can lead to hurt feelings. How do you apologize when
you've accidentally hurt someone you love?

_____

_____

_____

_____

_____

_____

_____

_____

_____

_____

_____

_____

_____

_____

# WOULD YOU RATHER?

## BSC Family Edition!

For each scenario, circle which one you would rather do if you HAD to choose!

## Would you Rather . . .

Do five loads of smelly laundry from Kristy's brother, Sam **or** sit next to him for every meal when he won't stop burping?

Attend Aunt Esmé's New Moon Share-a-mony **or** attend Liz and Watson's wedding?

Let Mary Anne's dad pick out your outfits for a week **or** listen to Claudia's sister, Janine, correct your grammar for a month?

NO!

Go on a shopping spree with Stacey's mom **or** learn to knit from Claudia's grandma, Mimi?

# OMG

Be an only child like Mary Anne **or** have lots of siblings like Kristy?

Cook a healthy meal with Dawn's mom **or** order tons of takeout with Liz and Watson?

Learn to code with Janine **or** play video games with Kristy's brother, Sam?

After Claudia's grandmother, Mimi, has a stroke, she has trouble communicating in English in the early stages of her recovery. She speaks to Janine in Japanese, her first language, and Claudia learns something new about Mimi's childhood. Claudia can't believe she didn't know something so major about the family member she is closest to.

Choose a family member—or a few—and interview them to fill in the answers below. You might be surprised at the stories you hear about the lives lived before you came along.

My interview with _____

They were born in _____

They grew up in _____

When they were little, they liked to _____

_____

_____

_____

One of their favorite memories is when _____

_____

_____

_____

Something I learned that surprised me is _____

_____

_____


My interview with _____

They were born in _____

They grew up in _____

When they were little, they liked to _____

_____

_____

_____


One of their favorite memories is when _____

_____

_____

_____


Something I learned that surprised me is _____

_____

_____

_____

With help from her friends, Mary Anne transforms her bedroom from an outdated little girl's room to a super-cool, grown-up space that feels much more *Mary Anne.* Think about what you would love to change if you could give your room a total makeover. Create a mood board by filling these pages with sketches or magazine clippings to inspire your dream sleep space!

## Stacey's Sea City Packing List

- ☐ Pink bikini
- ☐ Blue bikini
- ☐ Black bikini
- ☐ Black flip-flops
- ☐ Black Converse
- ☐ Nail polish—assorted colors
- ☐ White beach cover-up
- ☐ Black beach cover-up
- ☐ Cute hoodie
- ☐ Sunglasses—2 pairs (1 for each bikini, obvs)
- ☐ Toe ring (cute or passé?)

# Mary Anne's Sea City Packing List

- ☐ SPF 75 (two bottles—do *not* want a repeat of the Sunburn Debacle of 2019)
- ☐ Floppy sun hat
- ☐ Beach caftan
- ☐ Extra towels
- ☐ Sneakers
- ☐ Water shoes
- ☐ Extra socks
- ☐ One-piece swimsuit
- ☐ Warm sweatshirt—just in case
- ☐ The perfect beach read

# SEA CITY SURPRISE

**The beachside story has been started for you. It's up to you what happens next!**

    Waves crashing. Sun shining. Seagulls squawking. Okay, maybe that last part I could do without. But still, this was a perfect beach day. I'm not sure how I managed to get a baby-sitting job that includes a free trip to Sea City, but it sure works for me.

    A few feet ahead, I spot some of the Pike kids happily digging in the sand to create a trench around their sandcastle. Nicky is poking his plastic shovel into the sand again and again, frowning. Margo scoots over to help, pushing away sand with her hands. Suddenly she stops, her eyes wide. "Woah!" she shouts. "Guys! You'll never believe what we found!"

**STACEY:**

I get why Mr. and Mrs. Pike wanted us in separate cars to help supervise, but I wish we could be riding to Sea City together! How's it going over there?

**MARY ANNE:**

Not too bad. I am glad. The beach will be rad.

**STACEY:**

Um. What?

**MARY ANNE:**

Sorry. Vanessa has been speaking in rhyme the entire time and I think it's rubbing off on me.

**STACEY:**

Lol. At least you aren't in here with Claire, who barks at every car that drives by.

**STACEY:**

Oh hey! She's barking at you guys! Look out the window.

# What do you like to do during a long car ride?

_____
_____
_____
_____
_____
_____
_____
_____
_____
_____
_____
_____
_____
_____
_____
_____
_____
_____
_____

# MASH GAME, BSC EDITION

## What would your life look like in Stoneybrook?

Pick a number between 5 and 10. Starting at the beginning of the first category, go through the lists, counting each item until you hit your chosen number. Then, cross out whatever option you land on. Repeat this (skipping the crossed-out items) until you have only one option left in every category.

### Home

Watson's extravagant mansion
Esmé's mysterious manor
Claudia's funky bedroom
David Michael's tree house

### Romance

Logan Bruno
Trevor Sandbourne
Sam Thomas
Toby from Sea City

### Baby-sitting Gig

Buddy, Suzie, and Marnie Barrett
Bailey Delvecchio
Jackie Rodowsky
Jamie and Lucy Newton

### Hobby

Art
Shopping
Knitting
Sports

Write a little story about your future life, using the
results from the MASH game!

Ideas to Get Scott to Notice Me

1) Pretend to drown so he has to save me
2) LaCroix—a romantic offering?
3) Pretend to twist ankle
4) Casually run into him at the boardwalk
5) Pretend to get stung by jellyfish

What are some of the craziest things you would do to get YOUR crush's attention? Are they better or worse than Stacey's ideas? Do you think any of them would work?

1. _____

2. _____

3. _____

4. _____

5. _____

6. _____

7. _____

8. _____

9. _____

10. _____

Pick your craziest, most out-there idea for getting your crush's attention from the previous page. Now imagine that you actually did it—and it worked! What would happen next? Write a story about how you'd like your big romance to play out.

_____
_____
_____
_____
_____
_____
_____
_____
_____
_____
_____
_____
_____
_____
_____
_____
_____
_____
_____

Saturday

This has been the best Sea City trip EVER! My room is right next door to Mary Anne's and Stacey's. And they even ask me to help them with the other kids sometimes! I mean, since I'm 11 now, I'm practically old enough to be a baby-sitter on my own. I'm certainly more mature than the rest of my siblings. (Exhibit A: Today, Adam and Jordan put mayonnaise on Nicky's beach towel and told him it was seagull poop. It took me twenty minutes to convince him he could just rinse it off in the ocean and it would be fine.)

I hope Stacey and Mary Anne notice how good a job I'm doing. Maybe someday I'll be a member of the BSC, too!

Mallory

What's your favorite family vacation memory? Write about it here with as many details as you can think of so you never forget it!

# TOP 10 SLEEPOVER SNACKS

Finish this list the BSC members have started by adding your own favorite munchies!

1. Twizzlers —Claudia

2. Roasted chickpeas —Dawn

3. Potato chips —Kristy

4. Carrot sticks —Stacey

5. M&M's —Mary Anne

6.

7.

8.

9.

10.

# PLAN YOUR PERFECT SLEEPOVER ACTIVITY

Now that you have some yummy snack ideas, it's time to plan the rest of your perfect sleepover party!

Friends I'll invite: _____
_____
_____
_____

Music we'll listen to: _____
_____
_____
_____

Movies we'll watch: _____
_____
_____
_____

Games we'll play: _____
_____
_____
_____

The Importance of Decorum
By Kristy Thomas

Having "decorum" is all about behaving properly and following etiquette. I did not show decorum in history class when I pointed out that the phrase "all men created equal" is sexist and DUMB, but I was totally RIGHT and shouldn't that be the most important thing

Mr. Redmont, I know I did not show proper decorum when I interrupted you in class. Perhaps you now have a small taste of how all women feel when they are interrupted by men approximately 500 times a day.

Decorum is just another way to tell young women to act "ladylike" and enforce the patriarchal power structure our society has thrust upon us since our birth.

The Importance of Decorum
By Kristy Thomas

What is the meaning of decorum? Well, I know what it's supposed to mean. Raising my hand. Waiting to be called on. Being nondisruptive and all things that would probably make your life easier.

But to me, decorum means other things.

Like knowing when you're wrong.

Giving people the benefit of the doubt.

And most of all—being a good friend.

All in order to create a more perfect union, where all *people* are created equal.

Although it may not be *your* definition of decorum, it is mine.

Signed,
Kristin Amanda Thomas
President of the Baby-sitters Club

Sometimes we have to hold back what we really want to say—but not here! What have you been wishing you could say to someone if you didn't have to worry about the consequences? Now is your chance to get it all out!

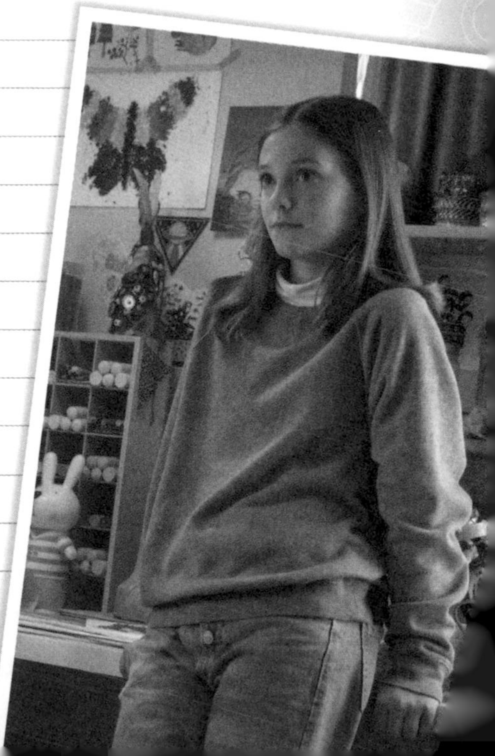

# WOULD YOU RATHER?

## BSC Friendship Edition

For each scenario, circle which one you would rather do if you HAD to choose!

### Would you rather . . .

| Have a heart-to-heart with Mary Anne | or | get some tough love from Kristy? |

| Redo your bedroom with Claudia | or | redo your wardrobe with Stacey? |

Think green!

| Join a protest with Dawn | or | start a new club with Kristy? |

| Attend a drawing class with Claudia | or | a theater workshop with Mary Anne? |

OMG

NO!

Have Stacey as a math tutor **or** have Kristy as a softball coach?

Go to Sea City with Mary Anne **or** visit California with Dawn?

Get a tour of New York City from Stacey **or** a tour of Camp Moosehead from Kristy?

CAMP Moosehead

Receive a painting from Claudia **or** a hand-knit scarf from Mary Anne?

Karen's TOP SECRET Spy Notebook

DO NOT LOOK—THIS MEANS YOU

OBSERVATIONS: MORBIDDA DESTINY

Day Three: Strange behavior continues

* 3:00: Gardening—probably ingredients
  for a potion

* 3:45: Unidentified package delivered.
  Maybe she ordered a new cauldron?

* 5:00: Many female visitors arrive.
  Members of the coven?

* 7:30: A fire in the backyard as darkness
  falls. What is it for?!

* 8:00: Daddy made me come inside. I'll try
  to get a good view from the window.

* 8:30: Being forced to get ready for bed.
  Observations must continue tomorrow.

# What's Your Secret Identity?

Karen Brewer is convinced her neighbor, Esmé Porter, is actually named Morbidda Destiny. Come up with your own mysterious secret identity using your favorite color and your Zodiac sign. Combine them in any order you like!

## Favorite Color

BLUE = Crescent
PURPLE = Midnight
PINK = Starry
GREEN = Solstice
YELLOW = River
RED = Sunshine
ORANGE = Goddess

## Zodiac Sign

CAPRICORN = Fortuna
AQUARIUS = Marvella
PISCES = Luna
ARIES = Amethyst
TAURUS = Magenta
GEMINI = Nebula
CANCER = Lavendula
LEO = Supernova
VIRGO = Ruby
LIBRA = Aqua
SCORPIO = Verbena
SAGITTARIUS = Aurora

# WHICH BSC MEMBER ARE YOU?

Take the quiz to find out which baby-sitter you're most like!

Your friends would most likely describe you as . . .

A. Creative

B. Sensitive

C. Glamorous

D. Confident

E. Determined

## What's your signature style?

A. A little out-there and totally original

B. Classic with a touch of modern

C. Trendy yet sophisticated

D. Cute and casual

E. Comfort comes before fashion

## What's your favorite subject in school?

A. Art

B. English

C. Math

D. Environmental Science

E. Social Studies

Where can you usually be found on a Saturday afternoon (if you aren't baby-sitting, of course)?

A. A drawing class
B. Getting cozy with a book and a cup of tea
C. Shopping
D. Volunteering
E. Playing sports

On a vacation with your friends, you would be the one . . .

A. Documenting every moment with your camera
B. Packing all the essentials (map, sunscreen, etc.)
C. Finding all the best restaurants and cafés to visit
D. Planning an outdoor adventure, like surfing or snorkeling
E. Making sure everyone sticks to the itinerary you've outlined

When you grow up, you'd most like to be . . .

A. A graphic designer
B. A teacher
C. A marketing executive
D. A yoga instructor/community organizer
E. A CEO of a major company

## Mostly As—Claudia

You love having fun with anything visual and creative. You're always expressing yourself through your accessories, clothing, and décor. No one else could pull off the truly unique style you have both inside and out.

## Mostly Bs—Mary Anne

You're responsible, organized, and, at times, on the quiet side. You speak up when it matters most, and your friends appreciate that they can always count on you to keep a cool head in an emergency.

## Mostly Cs—Stacey

You're always a step ahead of the newest trends. Your friends look to you for recommendations on anything from clothes and accessories to movies and music. You always know what's going on around town, and you get invites to the most exciting events!

## Mostly Ds—Dawn

You don't like to be boxed in, but if one thing is for sure, it's that you're at your best when you're taking action and helping others. You like to keep busy and make a difference in your community.

## Mostly Es—Kristy

You're a natural born leader, so your eye is always on the prize. You don't let distractions get in the way of achieving your goals. And after one goal is reached, you're ready to take on the next one!

# "I started the Baby-sitters Club to take care of kids. But what I didn't realize was that it was also to take care of me."

—Kristy

Everyone has embarrassing moments, including the members of the BSC. (Like the way Stacey got poison ivy all over her face at Camp Moosehead!)

**Confess your most embarrassing moment EVER. Your secret is safe here!**

!!!

# TOP 10 MOVIE NIGHT MUST-HAVES

Complete the list with everything you and your friends need for the perfect movie night.

1. Popcorn: classic AND fun flavors

2. Hot chocolate & marshmallows

3. Cozy pajamas

4.

5.

6.

7.

8.

9.

10.

# AND THE AWARD GOES TO . . .

Now that you're set with movie night supplies, it's time to hand out some awards! Fill in the list below with your top movie pick for every occasion.

Best Movie for Baby-sitting: _____

Best Sleepover Movie: _____

Best Home Sick from School Movie: _____

Best Date Movie: _____

Best Family Night Movie: _____

Best Movie to Watch Over and Over: _____

Best Holiday Movie: _____

Kristy was inspired to start the Baby-sitters Club after her mom struggled to find a baby-sitter for her little brother, David Michael. But baby-sitting is so much more than a job to the BSC. They care about the kids they watch over and know how much of a difference a baby-sitter can make in a kid's life.

Did you have a regular baby-sitter growing up? Who stands out as the person who has always taken care of you? Write about that person here.

My favorite baby-sitter was:
_____
_____
_____
_____

Our favorite thing to do together was:
_____
_____
_____
_____

My best memory with them is:

_____

_____

_____

_____

_____

_____

_____

_____

_____

_____

_____

One thing I'd like them to know now is:

_____

_____

_____

_____

_____

_____

_____

_____

_____

_____

_____

"Kids deserve fun baby-sitters who care about them. Who actually want to be there."

—Kristy

_____
_____
_____
_____
_____
_____
_____
_____
_____
_____
_____
_____
_____
_____
_____
_____

# Why do YOU want to be a baby-sitter?

_____

_____

_____

_____

_____

_____

_____

_____

_____

_____

_____

_____

_____

_____

_____

_____

_____

_____

_____

**DAWN:**

Code red. Code red. Earth to Mary Anne.

**MARY ANNE:**

Omg are you okay? Aren't you baby-sitting the Barretts right now?

**DAWN:**

EXACTLY! They're out of control! In much need of some guidance.

**MARY ANNE:**

Okay. I'm sure it's not as bad as you think. What's going on?

**DAWN:**

Marnie has not stopped crying/screaming. Suzi unrolled every single toilet paper roll in the house to "make a new dress." And Buddy just discovered that parkour is a thing.

**MARY ANNE:**

Yikes. Maybe it IS as bad as you think.

When is the last time you felt super stressed out?
What did you do?

_____

_____

_____

_____

_____

_____

_____

_____

_____

_____

_____

_____

_____

_____

_____

_____

_____

_____

_____

_____

Kristy is always coming up with great ideas to improve the BSC and make sure they're the best baby-sitting club around.

Come up with your own totally original million-dollar idea for how the girls could up their baby-sitting game! Would it be a weekly podcast sharing tips to fellow baby-sitters around the country? What about selling merchandise featuring their logo, like totes, T-shirts, and hats?

**The possibilities are endless and completely up to you. Make Kristy proud!**

# WOULD YOU RATHER?

## BSC Dilemmas Edition!

The BSC members have to make hard decisions every day. What would you do in their shoes? Make a choice for each scenario.

### Would you Rather . . .

A++

| Fess up to a failing test grade | **or** | pretend you passed with flying colors? |

OMG

| Snoop to find out the secret your friend has been hiding | **or** | wait and see if she tells you herself? |

| Attend an exclusive, world-famous art camp | **or** | an outdoor summer camp with your friends? |

Accept an apology from a friend who hurt you **or** hold a grudge for years?

NO!

Silently listen to a teacher say something you don't agree with **or** speak up and risk getting in trouble?

Call an ambulance in an emergency **or** wait for an adult to take charge?

Home    Today    Following

16
Candy Dessert
Recipes

THE LATEST
STONEYBROOK STREET
STYLE

The Artist's Ultimate Guide to Brushes

11 BABY-SITTING GAMES KIDS CAN'T GET ENOUGH OF!

The BSC members are best friends, but sometimes they still surprise one another! How well do you and your BFF *really* know each other?

Fill in the blanks below with your own answers AND the answer you think your best friend would write. Ask her to do the same thing on the next page. (No peeking!) Then compare your answers. Who knows who better?

|  | Me | My BFF |
|---|---|---|
| My Birthday | | |
| Favorite Color | | |
| Favorite Animal | | |
| Biggest Fear | | |
| Best School Subject | | |
| Biggest Pet Peeve | | |
| Favorite Movie | | |
| Current Crush | | |
| Hidden Talent | | |
| Dream Vacation | | |
| Favorite Food | | |
| Dream Career | | |

|  | Me | My BFF |
|---|---|---|
| My Birthday | | |
| Favorite Color | | |
| Favorite Animal | | |
| Biggest Fear | | |
| Best School Subject | | |
| Biggest Pet Peeve | | |
| Favorite Movie | | |
| Current Crush | | |
| Hidden Talent | | |
| Dream Vacation | | |
| Favorite Food | | |
| Dream Career | | |

**DAD:**

I haven't heard from you since this morning. When will you be home?

**DAD:**

Mary Anne. Where are you?
Answer me as soon as you see this.

**MARY ANNE:**

Whoops, sorry, Dad. I couldn't look at my phone while the lady was piercing my nose.

**DAD:**

WHAT?

**MARY ANNE:**

Kidding! Kidding! I'm at Claudia's! My phone was on silent so I just saw your texts.

**DAD:**

I think I may have just had a small heart attack.

"This may come as a surprise to you, but it hasn't been easy, Raising you alone. Most of the time, I feel as though I have no idea what I'm doing ."

—Richard Spier

_____
_____
_____
_____
_____
_____
_____
_____
_____
_____

Dawn and Sharon Decide:
Possible Names for Our New Pet Turtle

1. Ruthie (short for Ruth Bader Ginsburg)

2. Shelly

3. Sunny

4. Gloria

5. Is our turtle even a girl?

6. Though it shouldn't really matter because gendered names are a social construct.

7. Donatello/Leonardo/Raphael (too obvious?)

8. Speedy (This suggestion was from Mary Anne's dad, and while he's the one who gave us our new friend, we're not sure it's as hilarious as he thinks it is.)

Fill in the list below with your own favorite names for your dream pet!

1. _____

2. _____

3. _____

4. _____

5. _____

6. _____

7. _____

8. _____

9. _____

10. _____

# Official Baby-sitters Club Meeting Minutes

By Mary Anne Spier, Secretary

Meeting #22

Friday

In attendance: Kristy Thomas (KT), Claudia Kishi (CK), Stacey McGill (SM), Dawn Schafer (DS), and Mary Anne Spier (MAS)

## Jobs Booked:

* CK for Linny Papadakis next Tuesday
* SM for Charlotte Johanssen on Sunday
* NO members available on Saturday (tomorrow) due to the big Thomas-Brewer wedding!!!! Which isn't an issue because many of our clients will also be at the wedding, anyway.
* KT wants to run a "Kid Zone" at the reception where parents can drop off their kids, but all other club members convince her that's taking it too far considering this is HER OWN MOTHER'S WEDDING and she will have other things to do. (But possible expansion opportunity for future Stoneybrook weddings?)

## Other Points of Discussion:

* Charlie Thomas—New BMW
  — KT thinks it's too fancy but could be a big help to the BSC: free rides to baby-sitting jobs in a cool car!
  — Charlie not thrilled about this arrangement but seems like he has no choice.
* The Wedding
  — KT thinks it's too fancy (noticing a pattern here)
  — KT's bridesmaid dress remains a mystery to the club.
* Camp Mohawk
  — CK is planning to attend art camp at Yale with Trevor Sandbourne instead.
  — Packing lists have arrived! Let the countdown to camp begin!

PLEASE JOIN US TO CELEBRATE
THE WEDDING OF

## Elizabeth Thomas
and
## Watson Brewer

THEIR COMMITMENT TO EACH OTHER
AND THE JOINING OF THEIR
TWO FAMILIES INTO ONE

CEREMONY AT 4 P.M.
AT THE BREWER HOUSEHOLD

DINNER AND DANCING TO FOLLOW

The BSC members have added their top picks below. Complete the list with what you think would make the best wedding ever!

## Top 10 Essentials for the Best Wedding Celebration Ever

1. Drop-dead gorgeous wedding dress —Stacey

2. The perfect color skeem to tie it all together —Claudia

3. A romantic first dance for the couple —Mary Anne

4. Killer playlist for the reception — Dawn

5. Um, I don't really care about this stuff. Good cake, I guess? —Kristy

6.

7.

8.

9.

10.

LOVE

# RING THE ALARM

Not all weddings go quite as smoothly as Liz and Watson's. Help solve the wedding day dilemma below by finishing the story!

    After the hairdresser put the finishing touches on my curls, I looked in the mirror to examine the final product. I was pleasantly surprised. This was my first time being a junior bridesmaid, but I had heard hairdo horror stories from some of my friends who had been in weddings before.

    It was almost time for the ceremony to begin. All the other bridesmaids were putting their shoes on and getting ready to go outside. Then the maid of honor rushed into the room, her eyes searching around wildly. They stopped on me.

    "Please, please tell me you have the ring," she said.

    "No. I don't. Why?" I replied.

    "Because if you don't have it," she said, looking like her worst fears had been realized, "that means it's gone missing."

_____

_____

_____

_____

_____

_____

The night before her mom's wedding, Kristy finishes packing up her bedroom. Her family will be moving in with Watson's— and even though he has a beautiful mansion, that won't replace the home Kristy has grown up in.

**What is the one place that will always feel like home to you, no matter what? The place you've made countless happy memories with family and friends? Is it where you live now, or a place from your past? Revisit your favorite moments here.**

_____

_____

_____

_____

_____

_____

_____

_____

_____

_____

_____

_____

_____

_____

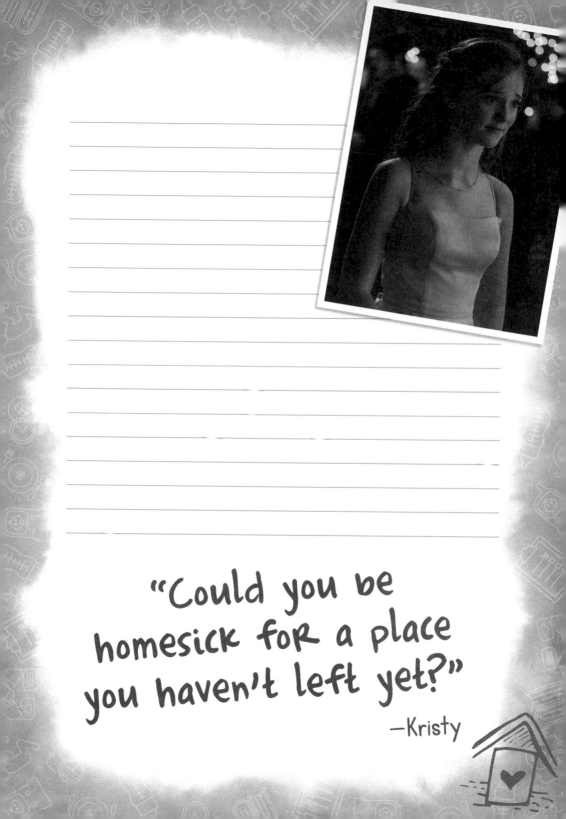

"Could you be homesick for a place you haven't left yet?"

—Kristy

At the end of the school year, the BSC members write messages in one another's yearbooks—and they find notes from a few other familiar faces, too! Check out some of them here, and then ask your friends to fill in the rest of the space with their own signatures!

Dawn,
I'm so happy you moved to Stoneybrook! You were there for me when I really needed a friend. And I have a feeling Project Parent Trap will have many successful missions this summer . . .
XO, Mary Anne

Claudia,
Thanks for helping me start the best club EVER this year! I have to admit . . . I couldn't have done it without you.

Kristy

Stacey,

Thank you thank you THANK YOU for getting me thru my math final. I owe you a pare of Claudia Kishi Original earings. Just let me know what color you want.

♡Claudia

Hi Mary Anne,

I heard you're going to be at Camp Moosehead this summer, too! I hope we get the chance to hang out. See you soon!

Logan

Claudia,

It was great having art class with you. I hope we're in the same class again next year! Have an awesome summer.

Trevor

# KRISTY'S CAMP MOOSEHEAD PACKING LIST

## <u>Camp Moosehead</u>
### Official Packing List—Suggested Items

☐ Camp uniform (available for purchase in advance on our website)
- ○ 5 camp T-shirts
- ○ 5 pairs camp athletic shorts
- ○ 5 pairs camp socks

*Definitely bringing my visor, too!*

☐ ~~Tennis racket.~~ *Softball and glove*

☐ Riding helmet (for those on the equestrian track)

☐ Bedsheets (long, 2 sets)

☐ Towels (2)

☐ Toiletry kit: soap, shampoo, feminine products, toothbrush, and toothpaste

*Should I bring just in case?? Mary Anne will probably pack extra.*

What would you bring with you to summer camp?

_____
_____
_____
_____
_____
_____
_____
_____
_____
_____
_____
_____
_____
_____

When Claudia and Dawn realize that not all campers are treated equally, Camp Moosehead activities don't quite go according to plan. Where do you think you would end up: performing in the musical with Mary Anne or joining the protest with Dawn and Claudia?

Choose one! Fill in the space on the next page with either a poster advertising the camp production of *Paris Magic* OR an attention-grabbing sign you could use to make your voice heard at the protest.

# "As much as I love camp, being your comrade has been the best part."

—Claudia to Dawn

> "Some say on quiet nights, you can still hear the vanished campers singing to him."
>
> —Karen Brewer

## The Curse of the Old Camp

The story of the hermit at Camp Moosehead is legendary.

Put your own spin on the campfire tale by adding to it below!

Old Camp is called Old Camp for a reason. Nobody goes over there—at least, they aren't supposed to.

The brave ones—or foolish ones, depending on how you look at it—who venture deep into the woods might not see much at first. Some abandoned cabins that have long ago fallen into disrepair. Maybe an old soccer ball or handmade wind chime forgotten by campers of years past.

But the deeper they venture into the woods, the more likely they'll come across him: the hermit. Watching. Waiting. Ready to cast another curse on any child who dares disturb his peace again.

Well, I promised you I'd tell you all about how camp went, but I didn't realize
I'd have something so big to tell by the end of it . . .

LOGAN AND I KISSED!!!!!!!!!!!!!!!!

And you would be very proud of me because I kissed HIM. Turns out he's
apparently pretty shy. Who knew?! But it helped that we were playing love
interests in the camp production of *Paris Magic*. (Which I also directed!
Though our opening night was a little, um, shaky because of . . . well, more
on that later.)

I have no idea what this means. Are we kind of dating now? How will he act
when we go back to school? How do I act when we go back to school????

Anyway, that's the big update from me. How's your summer going? Any
cute Sea City tourists catching your eye?

XO,
Mary Anne

Reply    A    📎    🙂    ⚬

**To** Mary Anne

**Subject** Re: The Latest from Stoneybrook

YOU KISSED LOGAN?? AND YOU DIRECTED AND STARRED IN A MUSICAL PRODUCTION?? When you told me about this camp, I pictured some marshmallow roasting and capture the flag, not the plot of a romantic comedy. I could have totally been there as the best friend giving you advice (but, in a twist: also while having my own whirlwind romance with a guy from a rival cabin). Maybe I'll get my parents to send me there next summer . . .

XO,
Alex

**REPLY**

Lawyer? World traveler? Mayor of Stoneybrook? Predict what you think each BSC member will be doing in ten years.

In ten years, Kristy will be _____

_____

_____

_____

_____

_____

_____

_____

_____

_____

In ten years, Claudia will be _____

_____

_____

_____

_____

_____

_____

_____

_____

_____

In ten years, Stacey will be _____

_____
_____
_____
_____
_____
_____

In ten years, Mary Anne will be _____
_____
_____

_____
_____
_____
_____

In ten years, Dawn will be _____
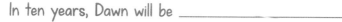
_____

_____
_____
_____
_____
_____

# Now it's your turn! What will you be doing in ten years? Dream big!

In ten years, I will be _____ years old.

I will be _____
_____
_____
_____
_____
_____
_____
_____

I will live _____
_____
_____
_____
_____
_____
_____
_____

I will still be BFFs with _____

_____

_____

_____

_____

_____

_____

_____

# WHAT'S YOUR BABY-SITTING STYLE?

Every member of the BSC is great with kids, but they each handle things in their own way. Take this quiz to discover your own personal baby-sitting style!

**You never arrive at a new baby-sitting job without . . .**

    A. Something to play with outside, like a softball glove

    B. An idea for a fun craft you can share

    C. A list of emergency numbers

**You're helping three kids make some cut-out cookies for their parents. You would most likely be . . .**

    A. Acting as the judge in a pretend baking competition

    B. Showing them how to make colorful icing patterns

    C. Leading them in an assembly line at the kitchen table to keep things running smoothly

**Your go-to move when a kid keeps misbehaving is to . . .**

    A. Enforce a "three strikes and you're in time-out" rule

    B. Make up a new game to sneakily trick them into following your instructions

    C. Start a reward system for good behavior

You're playing outside when a six-year-old trips and scrapes her knee on the sidewalk. It's minor, but she looks like she's about to burst into tears. What's your first reaction?

A. Tell her to walk it off—if you stay calm, so will she.
B. Show her your "magical healing powers" to distract her.
C. Whip out a selection of bandages and disinfectant to treat the injury.

Your favorite baby-sitting activities are always . . .

A. Active
B. Different every time
C. Organized

Mostly As—The Coach: You're firm but fair. You love to bring a little healthy competition to all baby-sitting activities and believe that sometimes tough love is the way to go!

Mostly Bs—The Creator: You have such a great imagination, it's almost like you're a little kid yourself—except that you also use your creativity to make sure your charges are safe while they're having fun.

Mostly Cs—The Coordinator: You're Super Sitter, prepared for any possible situation! You always think ahead and know how to make sure the kids have a good time without getting out of control.

"We were more than a club. We were best friends."

—Kristy